TO THE
FAIR

THE MAN WHO LOST HIS HEAD

THE MAN WHO LOST HIS HEAD

By Claire Huchet Bishop

Illustrated by
Robert McCloskey

PUFFIN BOOKS

PUFFIN BOOKS
Published by the Penguin Group
Viking Penguin Inc., 40 West 23rd Street, New York, New York 10010, U.S.A.
Penguin Books Ltd, 27 Wrights Lane, London W8 5TZ, England
Penguin Books Australia Ltd, Ringwood, Victoria, Australia
Penguin Books Canada Ltd, 2801 John Street, Markham, Ontario, Canada L3R 1B4
Penguin Books (N.Z.) Ltd, 182–190 Wairau Road, Auckland 10, New Zealand

Penguin Books Ltd, Registered Offices: Harmondsworth, Middlesex, England

First published in the United States of America by Viking Penguin Inc., 1942
Viking Seafarer edition published in 1974
Published in Picture Puffins, 1989
10 9 8 7 6 5 4 3 2 1

LIBRARY OF CONGRESS CATALOGING IN PUBLICATION DATA
Bishop, Claire Huchet.
    The man who lost his head / by Claire Huchet Bishop ; illustrated
by Robert McCloskey.   p.   cm.—(Picture Puffins)
Summary: When a man discovers he has lost his head he tries
several substitutes, but none is satisfactory.
ISBN 0–14–050976–3
[1. Head—Fiction.]   I. McCloskey, Robert, 1914–   ill.   II. Title.
PZ7.B5245Man 1989   [E]—dc19   88–28807   CIP

Printed in the United States of America by Lake Book Manufacturers, Melrose Park, Illinois
Set in Weiss Roman

THE MAN WHO LOST HIS HEAD

To
All my nephews and nieces in the Bishop family

Once upon a time there was a Man who lost his head.

He looked under his pillow.

But it was not there.

He got up quickly and looked under the bed. It might have rolled away.

But it was not there.

He looked behind the doors, and in the cupboard, and in the cat's basket.

But it was not there.

He even looked in the garbage can.

It was not ANYWHERE.

He sat down, and tried to remember.

It is very hard once you have lost your head!

Now, his hands remembered something soft and silky.

That was his pig.

And his feet remembered a long tiring walk.

That was the way to the fair.

So the Man came to know that much: that he had taken his pig to the fair.

Therefore the thing to do was to go back to the fair and look for his head there. Yes, that was the thing to do.

Only, of course, he could not go out like a headless fellow.

So he went into his vegetable garden. He picked a pumpkin. He cut holes in it and made a face. Then he put it on, and his hat on top of it. The hat was very small for such a large pumpkin head. But it was hardly the time to be particular! So he went out.

"Ah!" said the village people. "How well you look! You must have had a splendid time at the fair yesterday! You are flourishing! WE have not sold our pig yet. You are ahead!"

"I am ahead?" said the Man, distressed. "Ahead! Ahead! Did you say a . . . head?"

"What is the matter with you? Did you not understand?" asked the village people.

And they shrugged their shoulders, and turned their backs, and said to one
    another:

"The poor man! He must have lost his head!"

"Ah!" said the Man to himself. "This pumpkin head is too conspicuous."

    And he went back home in a hurry.

He rushed to his garden and he dug out a parsnip. He cut holes in it and made a face. Then he put it on, and his hat on top of it. The hat was very big for such a small parsnip head. But it was hardly the time to be particular!

So he went out.

"Ah!" said the village people. "How pale you look! All worn out. You must have had a dreadful time at the fair yesterday! Still, you sold your pig. That should be that much less of a headache!"

"A headache?" said the Man, distressed. "A headache! Headache! Did you say head . . . ache?"

"What is the matter with you? Did you not understand?" asked the village people.

And they shrugged their shoulders, and turned their backs, and said to one another:

"The poor man! He must have lost his head!"

"Ah!" said the Man to himself. "This parsnip head is too conspicuous."

And he went back home in a hurry.

He rushed to his woodshed and he took a log.
He carved a wooden head and made a face.
And he sandpapered it and polished it. Then
he put it on, and his hat on top of it. The hat
fitted perfectly.

So he went out.

"How do you do?" asked the village people.

And that is all they said to him, so like his own head was the wooden head.

So the Man went on to the fair.

When he arrived there he wondered:

"Now, let me see. Where shall I look for my head?"

Surely the pig market was the place. It was on the other side of the fair, and
the Man had to go through the whole fair grounds before getting to it.

What a hustle and a bustle! What a clatter and a hubbub the place was!
Everyone shouting his wares and calling from the booths: crockery lot-
teries, shooting galleries, bowling alleys. And the circus people parading
in tights on the platforms, the clowns turning somersaults, the wild beasts
roaring, and the merry-go-rounds grinding out their endless melodies.

The Man had not paid much attention to all this the day before, so intent was he on the selling of his pig. But now he was quite taken with the gaiety of the place. He went from one booth to another, bowling, shooting clay pipes. He threw rings around crockery pieces and was lucky enough to catch an elaborate shaving mug, which he took with him. He had a ride on a goat on a very fast merry-go-round. He admired the juggler and tightrope walker and finally decided to go and visit the wild animals.

There were lions, jaguars, leopards, and wolves, and, at the end of the row,
a beautiful royal tiger. He was stretched out, his left front paw care-
lessly dangling outside the cage, and he looked at the people across the
bars with a disdainful and bored expression.

"Hey, there!" called jovially the Man who had lost his head. "How are you,
Old Whiskers?"

And he leaned over and lightly struck the tiger's paw.

Instantly that paw was in the air making for the Man, who fell backward just in time. The people around gasped. The guard rushed in, furious.

"What are you thinking of?" he shrieked. "You! Silly fool! Idiot! Block-head!"

The Man was crestfallen.

"What were you trying to do?" went on the guard in a rage. "Have you lost your head?"

"Yes," said the Man sadly, "I have."

But no one paid any attention to what he said, because when anyone tells you: "I have lost my head," you really do not believe it.

Only everyone withdrew a little and let the Man pass and go out all by himself.

He felt very dejected and he sat on a bench trying to recover. He might have been killed by that tiger. It is dreadful what can happen to anyone who loses his head.

"Please, sir," said a boyish voice. "I heard what you told the guard of the menagerie. Is it true that you have lost your head?"

A Boy was standing in front of the Man. The Boy's hair was tousled, his pants hung from strings, his bare feet showed through the holes of his shoes. But he looked like a kind-hearted and very bright boy.

"Yes," answered the Man, "it is true. I wish someone could help me to find it. It is so very inconvenient. But no one believes me."

"I do," said the Boy earnestly. "And I think I can help you."

"Really!" said the Man, overjoyed. "You are the first understanding person I have met! But what makes you think you can help me?"

"Oh!" said the Boy. "I can. Because I am headstrong.

"Everybody tells me so.

"Now, sir, of course," said he, climbing on the bench next to the Man, "the first thing is to have a de-tail-ed-de-scrip-tion of the lost . . . object. That is always the way to start. What kind of a head did you have, sir?"

"A good one," said the Man.

"No use," snapped the Boy. "Everybody says the same thing.

First of all, how big? Like a pumpkin?"

"No, no!" said the Man hastily. "Ordinary size."

"And what shape?" asked the Boy critically. "Longish? Like a parsnip?"

"No, no!" said the Man hastily. "Rather round."

"Ordinary
    Round . . ." counted the Boy on his fingers. "Color?"

"Rather . . . pink. Yes, pinkish."

"Ordinary
    Round
        Pinkish. . . . Nose?"

"Hm! . . . A little bulbous."

"Ordinary
    Round
        Pinkish.
            Bulbous nose. Eyes?"

"Blue."

"What kind?" asked the Boy in a business-like way. "Ultramarine, indigo, periwinkle, cobalt, sky-blue?"

"Sky-blue."

"And were they hard or soft, shimmering like a friendly pool, or like cold
   steel?"
"I think they were soft and shimmering like a friendly pool. At least that's
   what I wanted them to be."
"Ordinary
   Round
      Pinkish.
         Bulbous nose.
            Soft and shimmering sky-blue eyes," counted the Boy. "We
            are getting somewhere."
"And the eyebrows were bushy and sandy-colored, and . . ."
"Wait a minute," said the Boy.
            "Ordinary
            Round
               Pinkish.
                  Bulbous nose.
                     Soft and shimmering sky-blue eyes.

Sandy bushy eyebrows, and?"

"Curly hair, much of it."

"Ordinary

   Round

      Pinkish.

         Bulbous nose.

           Soft and shimmering sky-blue eyes.

           Sandy bushy eyebrows.

             Opulent curly hair. . . ."

🦻 + 🦻 + 🦻 + 🦻 + 🦻 + 🦻 + 🦻 = 🦻

"You go in for big words," remarked the Man.

"I like them," said the Boy. "What about the ears?"

"A trifle too large," admitted the Man.

"Frequent," said the Boy. "Let me see:

    Ordinary
       Round
          Pinkish
             Bulbous nose.
                Soft and shimmering sky-blue eyes.
                Sandy bushy eyebrows.
                Opulent curly hair.
                   Average ears . . . average ears . . .

And what about the mouth?"

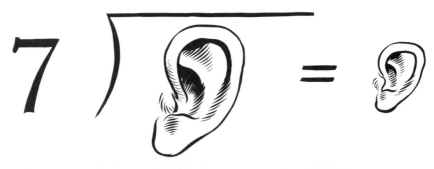

"Big enough!" exclaimed the Man gaily.

"And what about the teeth?" asked the Boy, almost severely. "They cannot be neglected!"

"All of them, and even, and healthy," said the Man proudly.

"Just what I thought . . ." sighed the Boy, "just what I thought! . . . And of course, no beard, no mustache, no whiskers. You shave."

"How did you know?" inquired the Man.

"Easy," said the Boy. "I can see that you chose a shaving mug for your prize. Now, let us recapitulate:

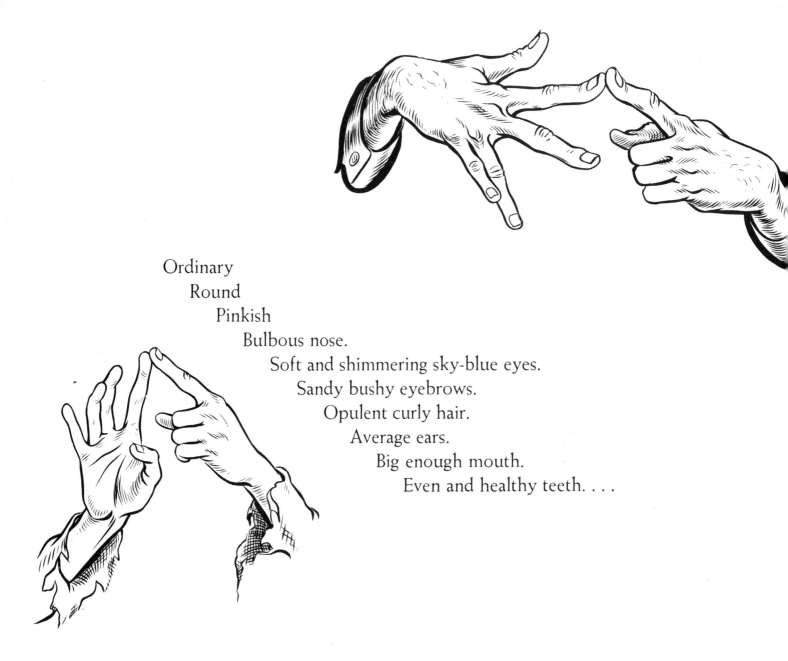

Ordinary
　　Round
　　　　Pinkish
　　　　　　Bulbous nose.
　　　　　　　　Soft and shimmering sky-blue eyes.
　　　　　　　　Sandy bushy eyebrows.
　　　　　　　　　Opulent curly hair.
　　　　　　　　　Average ears.
　　　　　　　　　　Big enough mouth.
　　　　　　　　　　　Even and healthy teeth. . . .

"Ah, sir," said the Boy sadly, "such a fine head! And you lost it. How do you
     think your head feels about it?"

"Badly," said the Man.

"That's just it," said the Boy. "So there is no use *looking* for it. A head like
     that cannot be found."

"What?" shrieked the Man.

"No," said the Boy. "We have to do something drastic. We have to conjure it back. I know all about it. I saw a magician once. There was a rabbit hidden in the audience, and the magician conjured it back into his hat. Only, one has to say the right word and make the right gesture. Then it all happens."

"All right," said the Man. "I am willing!"

"Sir," said the Boy, getting up and looking earnestly at the Man, "I think I know what kind of word and what kind of gesture I should use in this case. Only . . . you must understand . . . it is all for your good . . . and I would never do it if you had not lost your head. As a matter of fact, it is going to be pretty hard on me too," he added reflectively.

Whereupon he pulled pieces of rags out of his pocket and he began rolling
   them around his right hand. He held them tight, making a big mitt for
   his right hand. Then he said:

"Ready, sir?"

"Why, yes!" said the Man. "What on earth are you going to do?"

"BouliboulibouliboulibouliBANG!"

And the Boy punched the wooden head as hard as he could.
The Man saw a thousand stars. He felt dizzy and a sharp pain shot through
   his body.
He opened his eyes.

He was in his own bed.

And he had:

His

Even and healthy teeth.

Big enough mouth.

Average ears.

Opulent curly hair.

Sandy bushy eyebrows.

Soft and shimmering sky-blue eyes.

Bulbous nose.

His OWN

Pinkish

Round

Ordinary

HEAD!